The woman was crooking her finger at me to come closer, still standing on one foot. "Come on, fess up. You weren't looking for your cat, you were going to rip us off, right? You were hoping there might be something in there you could cash and carry, right?"

"No I wasn't!" I was moving closer to her, honestly insulted. What did she think I was? Behind her, through the partly opened door, I could see a room without furniture, cardboard boxes partly stacked one on top of the other and, upside down, against the back wall, a wooden stork.

My heart seemed to stop. I don't know what my face did, but it did something for sure. Maybe my eyes popped open and my mouth, too. Maybe I gasped. Whatever I did, it was a tip-off.

She was beside me before I could get my mind to accept what I had seen. She grabbed my arm and dragged me up the steps. One hand covered my mouth. I could see her face, grim, angry, not smiling anymore.

Mr. Riggs

Eve Bunting

Coffin on a Case

HarperTrophy
A Division of HarperCollinsPublishers

Library of Congress Cataloging-in-Publication Data
Bunting, Eve, date
  Coffin on a case / by Eve Bunting
    p. cm.
  Summary: Twelve-year-old Henry Coffin, the son of a private investigator, helps a gorgeous high school girl in her dangerous attempt to find her kidnapped mother.
  ISBN 0-06-020273-4. — ISBN 0-06-020274-2 (lib. bdg.)
  ISBN 0-06-440461-7 (pbk.)
  [1. Mystery and detective stories.] I. Title
PZ7.B91527Co 1992   92-855
[Fic]—dc20   CIP
                                                                AC

First Harper Trophy edition, 1993.

For Sam Spade—
with love

CHAPTER
ONE

My friend Paul and I were walking down Seventh Street toward my dad's office. It was June 18, and Paul and I were feeling fine. We'd each gobbled down two tacos and two orders of nachos in Burrito Belle's, the sun was shining and it was the start of summer vacation. We'd handled graduation from sixth grade, and it would be couple of months till we had to face up to the new terrors of junior high.

We stopped in front of 3411 Seventh. I pulled up the bottom of my T-shirt and polished Dad's brass nameplate, the way I always do. Not that it makes the nameplate look any better, and Mrs. Sypes, our housekeeper, says it certainly doesn't do much for my T-shirts either.

"You know, your dad should change his name," Paul said.

"What for? I'm tired of you telling me that. We like our name. It's unforgettable and very distinguished. It's also of old English origin," I said.

"Still." Paul leaned back and looked up at the redbrick building. "I'm telling you, this place looks like a funeral home. And then those names . . . Coffin and Pale. They could be two morticians. At least they should put 'Detective Agency' underneath. Nobody would ever know what they are from this."

"Lots of people know they're detectives," I said. That was an exaggeration, but it sounded good. "I gotta go now. My dad may need my help on a case," I added. "See you."

Coffin and Pale is on the second floor. I like the frosted-glass door with the two names arching across it like a black rainbow. That door is never locked. "We don't want to discourage a nervous client," Dad says. "Or any kind of client."

I walked in. Dad was reading the *Morning Star*, our local paper. He looked up. "Hi, Henry. Good lunch?"

"Yeah."

I can't wait till I'm old enough to be Dad's partner for real. Then we can be Coffin, Coffin and Pale, or just Coffin and Coffin, which would be even better. Not that I have anything against George Pale. He's a good detective. But a family business would be nice. I want to be like Dad, cool and tough. He always models himself after the detectives in old books and movies because that's what clients expect. Dad's favorite is Sam Spade, who is an old-timer and the best. We watch the video of *The Maltese Falcon* all the time. I just about know it by heart. I think it's because of Sam Spade that Dad wears a slouchy hat and sits with his feet up on the desk. He also has a belted raincoat, but it's usually too hot to wear it in L.A., so it hangs on a rack by the door.

I sat down opposite Dad in the client's chair, where I had a good view of the soles of his shoes.

"Anything happening?" I asked. He was reading THE POLICE BLOTTER, the overnight crimes report for our city. Sometimes we pick up a case from these reports.

"What's happening is somebody stole a truck with a house on its flatbed," Dad said. "The owners were having it moved somewhere, and the driver went in for coffee." He raised his eyebrows. "When he came out, no truck. No house."

"Wow!" I said. "Hard to hide. What else?"

"Somebody broke into a tropical fish shop on Del Mar and took three rare jewel fish."

"You don't think they're going to eat them?" I asked, horrified.

Dad grinned. "I doubt it. Not at two thousand bucks apiece. Kind of an expensive fish

4

dinner." He rustled the paper. "A thief made off with a jade figurine eighteen inches tall from the Eastern Asia Museum. *The Divine Scholar*, it's called. Ming Dynasty."

I looked over Dad's shoulder at the picture of the figurine—an old, bearded guy, probably green as a toad. He looked like a nice old dude.

"Worth about a million bucks," Dad said, folding the paper and scowling at the Dodgers' score. Sam Spade scowls a lot—at doors, at telephones. Dad just scowls at the Dodgers' scores.

"Pale called," Dad said. "I have to fly down to San Diego. He's having trouble with the insurance case and needs me. I'll probably be gone two or three days."

I sat up straight. "You mean you're going to leave me alone with Mrs. Sypes?"

"'Fraid so, Henry."

I groaned. Sypey's okay, but she's a bear about neatness, and bossy as can be. She's been our housekeeper for years and years, ever since Mom left, so she thinks she's in charge.

"Isn't there another case I can help out

with while you're gone?" I asked. "I could come in here, do paperwork . . . nose around about those fish, or that scholar guy. I bet a buck I could find that house. How many places can you hide a house, anyway?"

And that was exactly when someone knocked on the door. I turned in the chair and saw a figure outside the frosted glass, a definitely female figure.

She knocked again.

My heart beat faster.

I have two fantasies. The first is that some-day Mom will come knocking at the door and say, "I'm back. I lost my memory for twelve years, so I couldn't come sooner, but I found it again and here I am." My second fantasy is that a real gorgeous babe will come to the office and ask us to take her case. That's what always happens to Sam Spade and other de-tectives in old movies and books. In new ones too.

Dad says we've never had a gorgeous babe for a client. "Dream on, Henry," he says. "It's that kind of dream that keeps a person going." I wonder if he ever dreams about Mom coming back. Maybe. He never says.

"Come in," he called now. "Door's open."

I was still half turned in the chair, and I swear I felt my eyes bug out. This was one gorgeous babe!

She stood inside the office door, looking scared. I thought she was maybe sixteen, seventeen tops, which is, of course, way out of a sixth grader's league, even one who has already graduated. She was wearing a blue leather miniskirt and white boots and a white sweater that looked like bunny fur. Blond curls bubbled all over her head. Her eyes were big and blue and her lips cherry red. I felt as if I'd seen her somewhere before, but I couldn't have because surely I'd never forget a girl like this.

Dad stood up. "Please come in."

She took another step and felt behind her to close the door. "Are you Mr. Pale?" she asked in this soft, teary voice.

7

"No, Coffin. James Coffin. And this is my son and junior colleague, Henry Coffin."

"Oh."

It was when she said "Oh" and rounded her mouth that I knew where I'd seen her before—well, not her, but someone just like her. There's a very glamorous girl fish who swims around one of the Saturday-morning cartoons. She has these big eyes and foot-long lashes that she flutters and a red, red mouth. Her name's Cleo, and all the guy fishes go nuts over her. I don't blame them.

"Henry," Dad said gently, and I realized I was still sitting in a state of semistunment.

I jumped up and waved toward the chair. "Please sit down."

She stayed just where she was.

"I need a detective," she said. "Something awful has happened."

Dad came and took her by the arm and led her to the chair. "Why don't you tell us about it," he said. "Maybe we can help."

She sat and put her white shoulder purse on her lap. It had some kind of pop fastener and she kept opening and closing it, her head bent.

"My name's Lily Larson. And I've lost . . . I've lost . . ."

She gulped. When she lifted her head, I saw tears making little black makeup trails down her face.

I moved back behind the desk. Girls who cry do me in. Pearlie Withers, who sat opposite me in class, cried just about every day, and it made me crazy.

Dad slid a box of tissues close to Lily. "What have you lost, my dear?"

She dabbed her eyes and gave her nose a healthy blow. "My mother," she said, and began crying again.

I felt my own throat tighten in sympathy. Her mother! At least I couldn't remember losing mine, which was probably easier.

"Henry, get Lily a glass of water," Dad said, and I went gratefully to the corner sink.

"Where did you lose your mother?" Dad was asking her.

"She came home from one of her selling

days. I was at class. I'm taking computer science. Her car was in the driveway, and I thought, Oh good, Mom's home, and I let myself in. I called, 'Mom! I'm home.'" Lily stopped for another blow, looked around for a wastebasket and then dropped the used tissue into Dad's offered hand. Gross, actually. But it didn't seem to bother Dad. I gave her the glass of water, and she took a few sips. This nice flower scent hung around her like an invisible haze.

"So you let yourself in and you called 'Mom!'" Dad said. "But she didn't answer."

"No, she didn't." Lily shook her head.

I was having a little trouble with this. Had Dad let himself into our house all those years ago and called to Mom expecting . . . ? I glanced at him. His eyes looked sad, but I thought it was just because of Lily.

Lily popped the fastener on her purse open and closed, open and closed. "I decided maybe she was in the backyard or in her studio, so I didn't worry at first. When it got close to dinnertime, I went to look and she wasn't anywhere. I called her friend Jeanette in case the two of them had gone somewhere, but she wasn't there. And so I waited, and she didn't come home, and she didn't come home all night, and she didn't come home this morning, and I knew something was really, really wrong."

She stared at us and her eyes brimmed over. I wished I could clean her face up for her. She was going to be really upset when she saw it. Her lipstick was on her chin and her face looked as if it had been painted with zebra stripes. I swear, I know how it feels to be embarrassed like that. Once I'd gone the whole morning with a corn-puff kernel covering up my front tooth. I didn't discover it till I went to the boys' room.

"Have you called the police?" I asked Lily.

"That's what you should do," Dad said gently.

"I don't want to." Her purse pop, pop, popped.

Dad tried again. "But the police could—"

"Listen," she said. "You might as well know. I've lost my mom three times before. One of the times was just last week. I don't want to go to the police again."

"Three times before?" I sounded shocked and coughed to cover it up. "Excuse me." But she didn't seem to have even heard.

"I'm a worrywart. I admit it. There are just the two of us, just Mom and me, and . . . The first time I lost her, the car had run out of gas, and she had to hike to town to get to a phone and I'd already called the police. They were nice and everything. They were nice the second time, too." She blinked. "Last week what happened was, Mom left me a note by the phone saying she'd be very late and it fell, don't ask me how, and there were phone books, you know, a big bunch of them, piled on the floor, and the note slid down. . . . Anyway, I didn't see it. And she didn't come home and I called the police again."

Dad made a church steeple out of his fingers

and smiled across it. "That was exactly the right thing to do, Lily."

"They said maybe I should wait awhile," Lily said. "I mean, they were still nice and everything, but . . ."

"Could she have left another note?" I suggested. "Did you check under the phone books?"

Lily gave me a put-down look, which probably would have crushed me, except a put-down look doesn't work so well when a person's face is all mucked up.

"Mom and I have a new system," she said. "Magnets on the refrigerator. There was no note."

"Let's get this straight," Dad said. "Your mom came home, left her car in the driveway . . ."

"Left the bags of groceries in the car and the keys in the ignition, which she never does," Lily added.

"Went in the house and disappeared," I finished.

"How could she go in the house?" Lily asked.

13

"Her housekey was there in the car, with all the others."

"Maybe she went for a walk, or shopping," I suggested.

"All night? Give me a break, and if she did decide to go for a walk, wouldn't she put the groceries away first? There was frozen spinach. And then, this morning, I discovered one of her storks is missing."

"Her storks?" Dad raised his eyebrows.

"Yes. And so I know something awful has happened."

Dad was nodding as if he agreed, as if he knew the importance of a missing stork, which was more than I knew.

"Well, Lily," he began.

"Will you take the case? Please?" Lily asked.

My heart was beating like crazy. I felt as if I'd been struck by lightning. This gorgeous babe was asking us to take her case. My second fantasy had finally come true.

14

CHAPTER
TWO

It's sad when your fantasy gets blown away before you've had time to enjoy it.

"I'm sorry, Lily," Dad was saying. "My partner's in San Diego and he needs me. I'm catching the four-o'clock plane from Burbank."

Lily looked from Dad to me, then back at Dad. "What about him? Is he going too? I saw his picture in the *Morning Star* with you that time you foiled the jewel heist. 'Young detective works with dad.'"

I was pleased that she'd read the article, though actually I thought the reporter hadn't taken me seriously. And calling a stolen cat collar with a diamond in it the size of a spider's eye a jewel heist was a joke. But still, we'd had press coverage. And cute girls like Lily had read it. No complaints from this young detective.

Dad smiled. "That's true, but Henry's not exactly licensed to work on his own yet." He leaned across the desk. "I tell you what, Lily. Why don't *I* call the police for you? I have some pretty good friends in the department. They're really the ones who should be handling this."

Lily tossed her head and her blond bubble curls bounced. "Not yet. I'm waiting this one out a little longer. It's embarrassing—you know?"

"Well, what about another private investigator, then?" Dad started riffling through his card file.

Lily stood and smoothed down her little blue leather skirt. "I am capable of finding my own private investigator, thank you very much. I'm not helpless, you know. I found you."

"Wait a sec." Dad held up his hand. "Were you alone in your house last night? That's not a very good idea, you know, and—"

Lily interrupted. "I was not alone. I had Maximillian."

"Is he your . . . your . . ." I began, but I couldn't think who he might be, since she'd said there were just the two of them, just Lily and her mom.

"Maximillian is my dog," she said. "My very big dog." She looked me up and down. "Much, much bigger than you."

"Oh excuse *me*," I said, borrowing Paul's favorite expression. This girl was not only gorgeous, but sharp, too.

Lily made sure her purse was closed and hung the strap over her shoulder.

"Uh," I said, "would you like the key to the bathroom so you could . . . freshen up before you go?" I edged past Dad, yanked open his long desk drawer and took out the key. I swear, our bathroom key is so humongous you'd think it was to Death Row in San

Quentin. I held it up. "Four doors down the corridor."

"Thank you, but I'm in a hurry," Lily said in that same superior way. Wow, was she ever going to be sorry she'd been so superior when she got a look at herself.

At least she didn't bang our door behind her when she left. Dad and George Pale had one client do that and all the glass fell out.

"There goes a dream," I said, listening to the heels of her boots clumping down our stairs.

Dad grinned. "Kind of a prickly dream, huh?"

I flopped back into the chair. "She's worried. Do you think her mom's really lost this time?"

"I doubt it." Dad was sliding papers from the desktop into one of the drawers. "Rule Number Five in the detective's handbook: Most things have a logical explanation."

I don't think there is a detective's handbook. I think Dad just makes up the rules as he goes. "But where *is* her mother? And what was that about a stork?"

Dad stopped leafing through his desk calendar. "That's right. We never did get the exact story on the stork, did we? Too bad. Listen, Henry, I gotta go. But I don't like the idea of that girl being on her own. I think I'll call Jack Aquino from the airport and ask him to run over to Lily's house and check out what's happening." Jack Aquino is a friend of ours and an officer in the Pasadena Police Department.

"She didn't *tell* us where she lives," I said.

Dad struck the side of his head with his hand. "Oh man! I broke the first rule in the handbook. First off, always get the client's name and address. I'll call Jack anyway. He's got resources."

I could tell Dad wasn't too worried, though. He was taking his grungy old raincoat off the rack and saying, "You think I could use this in San Diego?" and answered himself, "Naw. Better to leave it."

19

We locked the door behind us and headed down to the parking lot. "Maybe her mom will be there when she gets home," I said.

Dad put an arm around my shoulders. "I'd lay a bet on it."

I nodded. But I wasn't all that sure, and I didn't know how he could be. We know of one mom who never did come back.

Dad dropped me off at home. He'd called Sypey, and she had his overnight bag ready. She had her warnings ready, too. Sypey has warnings for all occasions.

"I put in sun block and I want you to use it every day, Mr. Coffin. Even if you can't see the sun, it's there. And remember, wash off the toilet seat in your bathroom with soap and water, then discard the washrag."

"I will, Sypey. For sure."

"They try to deceive you with that strip of paper across the bowl." Sypey sniffed. "'Sterilized for your protection,' indeed. Most times it's not even wiped."

Sypey knows a lot of dark and dreadful truths.

"I put in your slippers," she told Dad. "Don't—"

Dad winked at me. "I know. Don't walk barefoot on a hotel rug." He wiggled his fingers. "Germs lurk and hide in hotel carpeting."

Sypey nodded. "Exactly. And I'll take good care of Henry. You don't have to worry."

"I won't." Dad took the bag, patted Sypey's shoulder and gave me hug. We walked down the path with him.

"Don't forget to call Jack Aquino," I said, and Dad said, "I won't," and climbed in the car. Sypey and I waited till he was gone.

I felt dejected as I followed her back into the house. Maybe it was because of the blown-away fantasy, or maybe I was just lonely.

Sypey, who knows me pretty well, offered me apple juice and oatmeal cookies in the kitchen. Sypey's okay.

Then I called Paul. He was sympathetic. "Too bad she got away. But you know what? There's no school again tomorrow. There's no school again for weeks and weeks and weeks. We're free." I could tell he was trying to cheer me up.

"Want to go to the P.C.C. pool tomorrow?" he asked. P.C.C. is Pasadena City College, and it opens its pool to the public every summer. "Robert Janek and Tony DeMeo are going. We could ride our bikes over and we could go to the library after. They're showing *20,000 Leagues Under the Sea.* Remember we saw it last year and there was that great octopus? We could get hot dogs in Jack in the Box for lunch in between."

I doubted that part. Sypey is not into letting me have hot dogs for lunch. "They've got preservatives," she says darkly.

"Want to?" Paul asked. "I need you to time me." Paul is determined to get first place in the underwater swim at the aquatics this summer. He got a stopwatch for Christmas and he's been practicing holding his breath while I time him. Sometimes his face turns blue. Paul is very determined.

"I'll ask Sypey and call you back," I said.

Sypey said okay to everything except the hot dogs. I was all set to call Paul back and tell him yes, but I had to take a sack lunch, when all my plans changed.

Lily phoned.

"How did you get my number?" I asked, astonished.

"How many Coffins do you think there are in the Pasadena directory?" she asked.

See? I thought. I'll have to tell Paul. There's another good reason to never change my name.

"Was your mom home?"

"No."

There was a long silence. I imagined Lily, next to that pile of phone books, standing in her white boots, the humongous Maximillian gazing up at her. Or *down* at her, if he was that big. I though of her pretty girl-fish face. By this time she'd probably fixed it up nice again.

"Will you help me find my mother?" she asked. "I don't think I can do it by myself."

I gave an excited hop. Good thing she couldn't see me. Hopping is not very cool.

"Well . . ." I was jazzed up all right, but a little nervous too. Okay to want to be a detective, but this might be serious stuff. Probably not, though. I reminded myself about Rule 5 in the detective's handbook, the one that said there was usually a logical explanation for everything. But still . . .

"How come you don't go find yourself another detective?" I asked cautiously. What I really meant was "How come you want a kid like me?" But I was smart enough not to put it that way. No use putting ideas in her head.

"I have very good instincts," Lily said. "My instincts today told me you were simpatico."

"Simpatico?"

"Understanding. Interested." She was right about that on both counts. I understand how rotten a person feels when a person loses a mother. And I sure was interested.

"It's almost six now. Too late to do anything. But I could come pick you up tomorrow morning," she said.

"You drive?" I asked.

"Of course I drive. And I have Mom's car."

I had a quick flash: Lily driving up, honking her horn, me dashing out, climbing in beside her. It might even be a convertible—red. I had another quick flash of Sypey dashing out after me, yanking me back out. Total humiliation.

"Listen, I have all kinds of leads," Lily said. "Serious leads."

"Did you find the stork?" I asked.

"The stork? No. I bet wherever they are, Mom and the stork are together."

I felt confused.

"Please," Lily said in a soft, small voice. "Please say you'll help me."

That "please" did me in. Not that there'd ever been any doubt.

"Okay," I said. "But don't pick me up. I'll meet you on Hill Avenue, right across from the library. You know where that is? By the college parking lot."

"Sure I know. At the back of P.C.C. That's where I take my computer classes," Lily said.

"What time?" I asked.

"Early. Nine o'clock."

"Nine o'clock," I repeated.

"Be there," she said. I heard the click as she hung up.

I'd be there.

CHAPTER THREE

Paul was mad that I wasn't going to the pool. "Who'll time me?" he asked.

"Robert or Tony," I said, slipping my small, black detective's notebook into my back pocket.

"I can't trust them the way I trust you," he said, which made me feel good. One of the things a detective must be is trustworthy.

Sypey thought I was trustworthy. She didn't suspect for a minute that I was going anyplace except the pool and the library.

I left a bit early so I could actually go to those two places and not be lying. The P.C.C.

pool wasn't open yet, but I stared at the blue water through the mesh gate and decided that was close enough. Then I chained my bike in the bike rack, took my sack lunch and went out to Hill Avenue to visit the library and watch for Lily.

The library wasn't open either. Sprinklers rainbowed on the grass, and a gardener in a fringed straw hat raked the rose beds. The dome of St. Philip's church gleamed gold in the morning sun. It was a peaceful scene. I sprinted up to the library door, pretended to read the notice that told the hours and stuck my hand through the "return books" slot. "I'm in the library," I said, and ran back to the sidewalk. Great, I thought. Sypey would be sure to ask, and she'd know in a minute if I lied. My conscience was clear.

Cars passed. None stopped. I worked at looking cool and sophisticated, which isn't easy without a slouchy detective hat and rain-coat and while you're holding a paper lunch sack with "Henry Coffin" written on it in black marker. Both sides. I decided to eat lunch and get it over with. I munched fast, dropped my empty sack into the "Keep Pasadena Beautiful" litter basket and explored my front teeth for peanut-butter deposits. That corn-puff experience had taught me a valuable lesson.

A car was stopping. It was red. It was not a convertible, but it was one of those neat old Chevrolet Impalas, long as a bus and with shark fins on the back. Driving it was Lily. I'd been almost on the money. Superb intuition is a great thing for a detective to have, and I have it for sure. With my intuition and Lily's instinct, I felt, we'd make a cosmic team.

My intuition had missed out on one thing, though. She'd brought the dog. He was sitting next to her and he wasn't big—he was gigantic . . . humongous! His coat glittered gold, like the dome of St. Philip's. His head was as big as a horse's. When he turned to look at me, his jowls swung.

Lily pushed on his rump. She leaned over and opened the door for me. "Hop in.

"Maximillian, get back," she ordered.

I waited carefully till the beast lumbered over into the rear, where there wasn't much room for him since sheets of plywood slanted across the floor and seats.

"Hurry up," Lily told me. "There's no parking here."

I felt like asking Maximillian's permission. He could take my whole head in his mouth if he wanted to, like a lion in the circus. I moved slowly, in case sudden movements made him nervous.

"Hi, dog," I said, settling into the seat, which was still warm from him. "Hi, Lily."

"Hi!" She gave me a dazzling smile. "Thanks for coming."

"You're welcome."

She had her hair pulled up on top and spread out like one of Sypey's feather dusters. Her lips were the same fire-engine red as the car, and her eyes had mysteriously changed color overnight from blue to grass green. I think it was because she had a lot of green junk on her lids. Probably yesterday the junk had been blue. What a neat trick! Only her lashes were the same, long and black and spiky.

Today she was dressed for jungle duty in a khaki shirt and shorts and the same little white boots.

"Your mom didn't come back, then?" I asked.

"No."

"Or the stork?"

"Or the stork."

"I'm sorry, Lily."

I fastened my seat belt and we zoomed off.

Behind me I could hear Maximillian's claws scrabbling for a hold in the plywood sheets. Just as long as he didn't sink them into the back of my neck.

We sizzled dead north on Hill. Ahead of us the mountains were romantically misted with morning smog. I was driving in a long, low-slung, lipstick-red car with a gorgeous blonde. It would have been picture perfect except for the monstrous beast of a dog. His drool was wet and cold on the back of my T-shirt.

"Good boy," I said. "Nice dog."

"Did I tell you my mom looks exactly like me?" Lily asked. "So keep an eye out as we drive. If you think you see me, it may be her."

"Okay." But it was hard to believe that any-one's mom looked exactly like Lily. I know lots of mothers, and none of them looks remotely like this.

We were heading straight for the foothills. Lily changed gears smoothly and silently. Wow, she sure could drive.

"Listen," I said. "I talked to my dad on the phone last night. He still thinks you should go to the police." No point in mentioning he'd also told me Jack Aquino was up in Sacramento, testifying against some druggie.

"Did you tell him you were on the case?" Lily asked, giving me a sideways glance.

"Well, no." I rushed on so she wouldn't ask why not, and why not was because Dad would probably have told me to stay out of it. "Dad says Rule Number Three in the detective's handbook is to work with the police, not against them."

Lily shrugged. "Last time I went to the police, they asked me if my mom had any boyfriends. Sure she does."

"I bet she does, if she looks like you," I said, very gallant and smooth. Sam Spade had taught me a lot of conversational skills.

"I told them yes, she has boyfriends. And I knew what they thought. They thought she'd gone off with one. They were wrong. But they would probably have thought the same thing again."

She gave me another spike-eyed look. "If we find we need the police, we'll call them. Meantime, we've got clues of our own and we're going to follow them all the way. Just the two of us. By the way," she said. "I forgot to ask your rates."

I tried to grin wolfishly, showing the edges of teeth far back in my jaw. Sam does that a lot. "Never mind the rates, babe," I said. "They're affordable."

She nodded. "Okay. But don't call me babe."

"Sorry," I said. She was right. Sam Spade's babes were dumb. I could tell Lily wasn't.

Now we were right up in the shadow of the mountains, turning left, paralleling the San Gabriels all the way. Lily swung sharply onto a small, second-class road that wound into a canyon. A sign said: THIS AREA CLOSED AT SUNSET. On another sign Smokey the Bear warned us sternly to help prevent forest fires.

"Doesn't this lead to Nunn's Trail?" I asked, turning to look at Lily and bumping my forehead against Maximillian, who had his back paws braced against the plywood so he could lean between us and gaze out the front window.

Lily eased around a rut hole. "There are houses back here too. We live in one."

"Oh." I pushed politely on Maximillian, who now was trying to climb over into my lap.

"Sit, dog!" Lily ordered. "He knows we're nearly home," she told me. "He's excited."

I was pretty excited myself.

Pebbles danced under our tires. They couldn't be very good for the red paintwork, but Lily didn't seem worried. Now she was stopping in front of a small wooden house. Maximillian launched himself over my shoulders, darn near smothering me before I could get the door open, looking stupid as he dashed round and round in circles in the dirt yard.

"He likes to go and he likes to come back," Lily said fondly as we both got out.

"What kind of dog is he besides big?" I asked.

"Great Dane."

I nodded. "He looks Danish." I hitched up my jeans. "Well, let's get a look at those clues."

Lily strode to the back of the car and opened the trunk. "See?"

I saw. The trunk was filled with neatly stacked plywood storks. Lily lifted one out and set it beside us. It was pale blue with a yellow beak and almost as tall as I was. A painted wooden baby dangled by its diaper from the beak. Two hooks stuck out of what I suppose was the stork's stomach, or maybe its chest.

Lily leaned back into the trunk and took something from a shoe box. It was an envelope-sized piece of wood with two holes drilled in the top. She hung it on the hooks. Painted on it in blue were the words: "It's a Boy."

I didn't know what to say or think.

Lily put the stork carefully back in the trunk and the tag in the shoe box.

"My mom makes these." She waved in the direction of the back of the house. "She has a workshop. She sells them."

I nodded. "She certainly is talented. So it's

one of these storks that's missing. I thought it was a . . . you know . . . a real . . ." I stopped, shamed into silence by Lily's look of incredulity.

"Give me a break," she said. "But there's a lot more to this. My mom keeps twenty of these big wooden guys in her trunk. I know she sold two yesterday before she disappeared. But there are only seventeen storks left. Count them."

I did.

Maximillian came to help me. I wondered what he'd found to eat since he came home. His breath smelled of dead rat.

"Seventeen," I agreed.

Lily beamed. "Exactly. And there are eighteen tags—one more tag than stork."

Maximillian and I counted again. I'm very good at holding my breath because I automatically do it while I'm timing Paul. Actually, I can hold my breath longer than he can hold his, but I've never told him. Actually, I could probably enter that underwater race and beat him, I can hold my breath so long. But I'd never do that. I am a detective and trustworthy. However, having this skill was useful now. While Maximillian and I counted, I didn't breathe at all.

"Eighteen," I said.

"Exactly." Lily pursed her mouth. "See?"

This was a *clue*? I scratched my chin thoughtfully.

"Come in the house and you'll see what else I discovered," Lily said.

I walked behind her. Her feather-duster hair went swish, swish, swish, from side to side. It reminded me of Sypey brushing cobwebs off the ceiling.

We went in a back door that led to an old-fashioned kitchen with white-tiled counters that sloped and a red-metal table with the kind of a hole in the center that holds an umbrella. There was no umbrella. But there were four red-painted chairs and red flowers that grew in boxes by the open windows. Talk about color coordinated. Everything shone.

Sypey would have approved.

Lily went straight to the table. "Here's the *Morning Star* that my mom left in the car. See the circles?"

The paper was open at the classified section, folded small. Two birth announcements were ringed with black marker pen:

> *Baby girl—Barbara Noser*
> *3432 Blue Ridge Road, Pasadena*
> *Born 6/6/92*

> *Baby boy—John Matthew Migran*
> *243 Cedar Lane, Pasadena*
> *Born 6/7/92*

I read them twice. "A boy and a girl," I said.

"My mom checks the birth announcements, looks up the ones that are close to us or easy to find, goes off in her car . . ."

"With the twenty storks," I added. "And the baby tags. Ten of each kind, which she keeps in the car trunk."

Lily nodded. "She hangs 'It's a Boy' or 'It's

a Girl' on the hook, goes up to the door and usually makes a sale. New parents are kind of sappy and extravagant, and they want to share the good news. They can set the stork on the porch or front lawn."

"Wow!" I was impressed. It was the kind of an idea that Paul and I were always trying to dream up and never could.

"Of course, Mom also advertises in baby magazines."

"So you're thinking she sold two storks, but where is stork number three?"

"Right. And why didn't the tag go with it?"

"Maybe she went somewhere she didn't circle in the newspaper."

"No. My mom plans ahead. She picked up the plywood, went to Blue Ridge Road, Cedar Lane, the market . . . all those places are in the canyon. She's careful of mileage. The Big Red eats up gas."

I believed it. Back in the days of mile-long cars with shark fins, gas probably cost a dime a gallon.

"Anyway, I know for sure where she went because of her mileage book. She keeps strict records for taxes." Lily took a notebook from the top of the refrigerator. "Mom clips this in her car behind the sun visor. Take a look."

There were columns of figures and writing. It was all there. I flipped to the last page. "No ending mileage."

"The odometer in the car registers 13262," Lily told me. "That means she drove twenty-eight miles and that's right, if she came straight home. But where did she go afterward? And she never sells a stork without a tag unless . . ."

She was waiting for me to finish the sentence. I almost panicked. What? What? Then I got it. "Unless she wasn't sure if the new baby was a boy or a girl."

"Right," Lily said. "A birth announcement always tells the sex. Sex is very important."

I know Sam Spade would have leered at a remark like that. But I don't really know how to leer, and besides, it wouldn't seem right at a time like this.

I pulled out one of the red-painted metal chairs and sat to think over the clues we had. "Rule Number Five in the detective's handbook says there's a logical explanation for almost everything," I told Lily, but not too forcefully, because this was fun—fun and fantasy—and I didn't want her to think the explanation, whatever it was, was so easy and logical she could figure it out without me. "Maybe she had a friend who had a baby and she went to the hospital and took—"

Lily interrupted. "And walked, carrying the stork? And left the groceries to melt in the car? And never told me? And never came back?"

"Then there's this." Lily took down a small white envelope that had been with the book on top of the refrigerator. "Look inside."

Inside was a squashed, dirty blue blossom. "Um." I nodded wisely. "Er, what exactly is it? A flower?"

"It's from a jacaranda tree," Lily said. "Its flowers drop all the time."

I nodded again. What the heck was she getting at?

"I found it in Mom's car. On the driver's side. It was trampled into the mat. I think it came off the sole of someone's shoe."

I got it. "You don't have a jacaranda tree."

"No."

I pondered. "But your mom could have walked on it at . . ." I glanced at the newspaper. "When she stopped at Blue Ridge Road or Cedar Lane."

"Maybe," Lily said. "Or maybe someone else accidentally left it in the car. Someone who was driving."

I looked up and saw the way her face was crumpled and how her cheeks were starting to get zebra striped as she cried, the way they'd done in the office. And suddenly it wasn't fun and fantasy anymore. It was sad and scary and serious. Of all the detectives in the world, I ought to understand that. Besides, my famous intuition was giving me strong signals. Something was defi-

43

nitely wrong here.

I pushed back the red chair, gave her the jacaranda envelope and stood up. "Okay," I said. "Enough of the talk. Let's you and me get seriously down to business."

CHAPTER
FOUR

"I'll check the vehicle first," I told Lily and Maximillian, opening the car door. "We *should* check for fingerprints. There's an ultraviolet imaging system now that intensifies light and shows up prints that are hardly even there," I added.

"You have one of those?" Lily looked impressed.

"No."

I slid in behind the wheel. Man, what a machine! It took all my willpower not to go *"Vroom, vroom"* and lean from side to side. Luckily, I have a lot of willpower.

Maximillian and Lily put their heads in through the open window.

"Let's go over this again, Lily," I said. "The blue flower was on the floor—driver's side."

"Yes. The jacaranda," Lily said.

"The two bags of groceries were still in the passenger seat, right?"

Lily and Maximillian both nodded.

"And the backseat had these big sheets of plywood leaning across them?"

They nodded again.

I frowned to show my concentration. "That means there was only one person in the vehicle—the driver. And when you got in, Lily, after . . . after your mom disappeared . . . did you have to move the seat forward or back?"

"No," Lily said. "The seat was right where it always is. My mom and I are the same height."

I opened the glove compartment. Maps and registration papers were neatly banded together. There was a comb, a lipstick and a dollar bill. "The motive was not robbery," I said. I pulled down the sun visor.

46

"Her mileage record was there," Lily said, "before I took it in the house."

I flipped the sun visor back up. It was slowly dropping again.

"It falls down. You have to stick the edge behind that strip of chrome," Lily said.

I did.

The car radio almost blasted me out of the seat when I turned it on. Quickly I fumbled for the volume knob.

"That's Billy Idol—'Rock the Cradle of Love,'" I said.

Lily's face had gone very pale and her spiky eyelashes quivered. "My mom would never listen to that. Never. She's classical all the way."

"Did you touch it?" Lily shook her head. "Then somebody else changed the station." Our first real clue!

"So somebody else *did* drive her car and left it here?" Lily asked in a low voice. "Probably the jacaranda person?"

I nodded. I couldn't look at her, she sounded so upset.

When I opened the car door, Maximillian

was so delighted that he knocked me back on the seat. Lily pulled on his collar. "He likes you," she said.

"Good. But where was *he* when some stranger drove your mom's car in here and got out? Why didn't Maximillian eat him? Or does he like everyone?"

"Of course not. He was locked in the house. We can't leave him outside. He follows the car. Mom used the take him when she went out selling storks, but the customers wouldn't open their front doors." Lily patted his head. "I bet if some stranger did come, Maxie barked real hard."

"Big deal," I muttered, looking at the high, sun-dry mountains that surrounded us, the empty canyon.

I prowled across the yard. If there had ever been footprints, they were gone—and no wonder, the way Maximillian dashed around in circles playing puppy dog.

I searched the yard at a crouch all the way to the road. "Hopeless," I muttered, and then I saw the tire tracks. I bent over them and had barely time to click one mental picture before the dumb dog came at a gallop to land splat in the middle of the tracks, leaving me nothing but skid marks. Quickly I whipped out my detective's notebook and drew the design before I could forget it.

It was very distinctive—three fat *S*'s curled together, a space, then three more, like sleeping snakes. "Normally we'd make a cast of these for the lab," I told Lily, who'd come to look over my shoulder. "But . . ." I flicked a thumb toward Maximillian.

"And look at this!" Just behind where I'd found the tire tracks were three drops of oil, each one the size of a quarter, in a straight line. I measured between them with my bent knuckle. "One inch," I muttered. "Important question. Who comes out here and parks on your property just off the road?"

"Nobody," Lily said.

"The mailman?" I asked.

"He comes all the way to the letterbox by the porch."

"Plumber? Electrician?"

"Are you kidding? You think we're rich?"

I touched the oil with a fingertip. It was wet and sticky. "Somebody stopped right here. And not that long ago."

"I don't get it," Lily said.

"Whoever brought your mom's car back had to get home. It was too far to walk. So someone else followed in another car."

"You mean there were two people?" Lily's spiky lashes quivered.

"I'm almost sure."

"You are very logical." Lily sounded impressed all over again.

"A detective has to be," I said. "Let's take a look at your mom's studio now." Sam Spade would have been proud.

"Maximillian isn't allowed to come with us. He's banned from the studio." We locked him in the house, where he proceeded to have a barking fit.

Lily led the way. The studio had been a small, rickety garage, not nearly big enough to hold Big Red. Sunlight came through the chinks in the roof. It smelled of wood shavings, varnish, paint. Plywood storks, finished and unfinished, leaned against the walls. I pried the lid off a can of paint.

"Angel pink," Lily said. "For a girl."

"Your mom does nice work." I ran my fingers along a template that lay on the workbench. "If I had a baby, I'd buy one these storks myself. Honest."

A small radio sat on a shelf. I turned it on and soft, classical music filled the studio. Somewhere up on the roof a mockingbird joined in. Maximillian's barks changed to howls.

"Mozart! My mom likes Mozart." Lily burst into tears.

"Oh no!" I turned the radio off and put my arms around her. It felt strange. In the first place, except for the time Pearlie Withers and I were in the Thanksgiving play and I was supposed to be her husband, I'd never had my arms around a girl. And that was awful because Pearlie Withers had a cold and her nose was dripping yuk, and I was scared some of it would get on me. And she smelled of cough medicine. Lily smelled nice. And there was a very exciting softness under her khaki shirt. I knew because that's the height my head came to and my cheek was against the soft part. I stood stiffly and tried not to lean.

The storks watched us with their smiling eyes, and all those little painted babies peeked out at us from their dangling diapers. Lily held me and sobbed her heart out. I patted her back . . . actually her waist. I guess my mother probably held me when I was little. I thought I had the memory of one time, and I had asked Sypey.

"Did we use to have a rocking chair?" The creaking of the chair was in my memory, and a woman singing.

"Yes," Sypey said. "It was in my room, but the seat needed to be recaned so your dad gave it away to the Goodwill and got me that nice recliner. Fancy you remembering that old chair, Henry."

"I thought my mother rocked me in it and sang to me," I said.

"No, love. I used to pick you up at night when you fussed, and we'd sit in the dark. I don't think you could remember your mother, Henry. You were only six weeks old when she left."

Sometimes Sypey's voice can be so soft and sad.

"I know I was only six weeks old," I said crossly. "I knew that. I just thought I remembered is all."

I never asked about the rocking chair again.

My ear seemed to be stuck to Lily's front. I must have relaxed while I was thinking about Sypey and the rocking chair, and I'd sweated us together. I tried to ease away gently without disturbing her too much. Her sobs were definitely quieter now. I waited. Sometimes she'd shudder, and we were so close that when she shuddered, I'd shudder too. It was pretty nice. Her hands clutched at my back. I'd tell Paul, "Her hands clutched at my back."

"Wow," he'd say. "A sixteen-year-old girl clutching at your back!"

She was whispering into the top of my head now. Thank heaven I'd shampooed with Peppermint Zing this morning in the shower. How gross if I'd smelled greasy.

"I'm just so scared," she said, turning away from me and taking a clean rag from a pile of folded ones on the workbench. She blew her nose. I hoped she didn't notice the sweat mark from my head on her shirt.

"Thanks for letting me cry, Henry."

"You're welcome. You can cry on my head anytime." I meant it, seriously.

"What's our next move?" she asked.

"If you feel up to it, we'll go in the house and think."

She blew her nose again. "I feel up to it."

I opened the door and stood back so she could go first. Sam Spade is not always polite with the ladies, and that's the only thing about Sam that my dad criticizes.

Maximillian was barking his brains out

again. "He wants to be with us, you see," Lily explained. "Maxie—we're coming."

We were passing Big Red. I laid an admiring hand on the red fender and glanced in through the open window.

"Didn't I put the sun visor up after I looked behind it?" I asked. "And didn't I slide that edge under the clip so . . ."

"Yes," Lily said.

"Sh!" I looked down. In the dirt by the driver's side door was a footprint. I put my hand on Lily's arm. "Don't move," I whispered.

I turned my head and eagle-eyed the yard and the front of the house. Maximillian was still barking. The same noisy bird twittered on the studio roof. I leaned over to examine the footprint. It could have been made by a tennis shoe, big, size ten or eleven. There was part of another one behind it and behind that something else. Sleeping snake tracks. And between them three drops of oil in a single straight line.

No jacaranda flower, though.

"Someone came while we were in the studio," I whispered. "He drove here in the same car, checked behind the sun visor. He knew what he was looking for."

"The mileage record," Lily said.

I nodded.

"When he didn't find it, he may have tried to go in the house, but Maximillian was there."

"Good dog," Lily said automatically. She grabbed my hand. "Henry! What if he's still here? Somewhere, hiding . . . at the back or . . ."

"Uh-uh." I pointed. "See where the tracks curve? There's where he turned back onto the road. He's gone."

Lily shivered. "How awful if he'd come in the studio!"

"He probably thought it was just a run-down old garage and not in use. And it was very quiet after I turned off the radio."

Lily's eyes were wide with fear. "But who

would know about the mileage book except Mom? Unless she told someone. Or . . ." Her sudden smile was like sunshine. Corny, I know, but true. "Maybe Mom's back. Maybe somebody drove her here and dropped her off. Mom! Mom!" She was racing toward the house, her little white boots kicking up dust all around her.

I followed slowly. If her mom was here, why was Maximillian standing by the window and still barking? Who had come? What was so important about that mileage record, and had someone forced Lily's mom to tell where it was kept? It wasn't a nice thought.

CHAPTER

FIVE

I wish I'd been wrong, but I wasn't. Lily's mom wasn't in the house. Lily stood by the table, head drooping, hands clenched on the table's edge. I wondered if she'd like me to hold her again. Probably not. So I just said, "It's awful to get your hopes up and have them smashed. That's happened to me a few times." Like when I came home once and saw a man in our bushes, setting up a ladder. Wow, a burglar, I thought. The nerve of him in broad daylight!

I tackled him at the knees. The ladder fell, but he didn't. He grabbed the front of my T-shirt.

"What's your problem, kid?"

Turns out Sypey had hired him to wash windows.

"Never, never do that again without informing me," I told her. "A detective's suspicions are easily aroused." And a detective is easily embarrassed, though I didn't tell her that.

I picked up the small, battered mileage book that lay on the table and began leafing through it. "Do you have a map of Nunn's Trail and the canyon?" I asked.

Lily wiped her eyes, nodded and went to get it.

Using the map and the mileage record, we plotted her mom's route. I noted it in my detective notebook. Her mother had detailed everything.

FIRST STOP: LUMBER YARD

(2) 3432 BLUE RIDGE ROAD

(3) 243 CEDAR LANE

(4) THE SAV-A-LOT MARKET

Lily calculated. "There's nothing extra. Mom just came back direct."

"Don't get upset," I told her, "but I think whatever happened, happened between the Sav-A-Lot Market and here. Logically we should go there first. But my dad would say that was sloppy. We should retrace your mother's route and see if we can pick up any information. Sam Spade would do that next too."

"I thought your dad's partner's name was Pale?" Lily said.

"It is. Sam's another private eye we know. But Lily?"

"Yes?"

"It should be the police doing this."

"No!" Lily ran her finger along the yellow line we'd drawn on the map. "Suppose my mom *doesn't* come back for a while and the police know . . . I don't think they'd let me stay out here by myself. There are probably places they make you go if you're sixteen. I mean, *I*

60

know she's coming back. She loves me. But . . . please, Henry."

"All right, we'll leave the police out of it for now," I said.

Lily flashed that smile on me again. I swear, that smile could melt the Hubbard Glacier.

"Let's go," I said.

Lily drove. I had the map spread across my knees. We'd locked Maximillian in the house, and behind us his frantic barking grew fainter and fainter. It was one thirty in the afternoon. By now, Paul and the other guys would be shoving their way into the library for *20,000 Leagues Under the Sea.* High adventure. But not as high as this.

We were driving along a narrow road between mountains that loomed purple and black. Lily slowed for a startled-looking squirrel that was crossing in front of us. I stole a sideways glance at her. She'd taken off the old makeup and put on a bunch more. Her feather-duster hairdo was gone, and tufts of hair stuck out all over her head like spokes on a wheel . . . very mod-looking. One thing worried me. She'd changed into a dress, or maybe an extra-extra-long black T-shirt. Right in the front, where my sweat mark had been on the khaki shirt, was a jaguar's head in gold glitter. Its eyes were two sparkly green dots. What if we met a bunch of hunters up here in the wilds? Should I mention the dangerous possibilities?

"Here's Joe's Lumber," Lily said.

We parked Big Red and went in.

Joe remembered Lily's mom and that he'd put the lumber in the back of the car.

"Well, we didn't find out much," Lily said when we left, and I had to admit she was right. She swung onto Blue Ridge Road. Up, up, up we went. Below us lay Pasadena, glamorous and misty. I could see city hall and the top of First Interstate Bank. The road was as narrow as tape. I crossed my fingers that we wouldn't meet a truck or an oil tanker, but all we met was a cyclist who waved cheerfully as he passed. I bet he wasn't that cheerful on the way up.

A stork with a dangling "It's a Girl" sign smiled at us from the lawn of 3432 Blue Ridge. There wasn't a tree in sight, jacaranda or otherwise.

I instructed Lily not to stop directly in front of the house for security reasons. "We shouldn't approach the door together, either," I said. "One of us should be here to go for help in case of an emergency."

"Well, then, I'll have to stay. You can't drive," Lily reminded me.

"I *could*," I said.

"Have you ever?"

"No. But I bet I could."

"We'll stay together," Lily said.

"I make the decisions," I told her. "I'm the detective on the case."

"And I'm the employer," Lily said. How could I argue?

Mrs. Noser came to the door holding a screaming bundle of blankets. I guess the baby was hidden inside.

"Oh, hi!" She gave Lily a tired smile.

"I'm the stork lady's daughter. We came to see if the stork was satisfactory," Lily said. "You didn't want to return it or anything?"

Mrs. Noser smiled weakly. "No. But how about if I return the baby? Only kidding."

"We were wondering if perhaps you bought two storks?" I asked quickly. "There's one missing."

"Why would I buy two? I don't plan to have any more babies."

We thanked her and left.

"At least we know she was safe this far," Lily said.

"Right." I checked the Nosers off the list.

I checked off the Migrans, too, after we talked to them and after we'd cased the property for flowery foliage and found nothing blue. "You can bet the trail's going to get hotter when we hit the market," I told Lily apologetically. I was hoping she didn't think she had hired herself a dud detective.

The checker in Sav-A-Lot knew Mrs. Larson. "*I* put her groceries in the car, in the passenger seat," the box boy added. He had brown hair, shaved on the sides and thatched on top, and he was very interested in Lily's jaguar.

"We're anxious to find out . . ." I began.

"Mom's disappeared, Jer," Lily whispered.

Jer whistled. "You mean she's taken off? Left you all alone?"

I pushed myself between him and Lily. "She's just gone away for a while. I'm looking after things."

The guy ignored me. A speck of green glitter had dropped off the jag's eyes. Jer picked it up with the top of his finger and held it toward Lily. "You want me to come by and keep you company, Lily?"

I was ready to punch him between his bulging eyes.

"Not even for a second," Lily said coldly. It was nice to see how well she could look after herself. Sam Spade and I admire women like this.

"Change your mind, let me know," Jer told

her, dropping a bag of grapes into a sack and tossing a can of stewed tomatoes on top.

"Did Mrs. Larson sell anyone a stork while she was in here?" I asked.

Jer tittered. "I've seen our customers buy chickens, turkeys and even rabbits, but no storks."

The checker stopped ringing up groceries. "Can't you see Lily's worried, Jer? Cut out the funny stuff. There was something, Lily."

My ears tingled. Dad always says a detective puts up with a lot of garbage because there may be a nugget of gold buried underneath. I had a feeling I saw real gold glinting.

"I did tell your mom about how a developer bought a bunch of those old houses down on Chaparral Road and fixed them up. Some young couples have moved in." He shrugged. "Maybe there are some babies."

"Thanks a lot," I told the checker. I felt terrific.

"Chaparral Road is on the direct route back to our house," Lily said.

"We're onto something, Lily," I said as we headed back to Big Red.

"Do you really think . . ." Lily began.

I rubbed my hands together. "It's a good possibility she went by, saw some signs of someone with a baby and . . ."

Lily interrupted. "But why would Mom stay? Something must have happened—something awful. I'm scared."

We stood looking at each other, and suddenly I was scared too. "We will find your mother," I said. "And we will proceed with extreme caution." It would have sounded more positive if my voice wasn't shaking.

CHAPTER
SIX

"We'll stop at every house," I told Lily. "I'll go up to the door and pretend I'm selling chocolate for my school."

"But it's summer. And you don't have any chocolate."

"You're right." It was good to have a smart partner. "I'm taking orders for fall," I said. "But what I'm really doing is keeping my eyes open for clues . . . baby signs, snake tire tracks, a size ten or eleven footprint. A stork. Anything suspicious, like a blue tree. We'll have a signal. If I whistle, it will mean something's gone wrong and you should go fast and bring the police. No, wait." I'd forgotten that I can't whistle. "I won't whistle. I'll cluck like this." I clucked.

Lily looked doubtful.

"It'll work," I said.

"But a hen? Up here? Won't that sound suspicious?"

"It wasn't a hen. It was a woodchuck."

"So if you cluck, I come and—"

"No. No. No. You *go*, fast as you can. You know where the police station is, up there by the city hall?"

Lily nodded.

"Also, if I don't come back in a reasonable time, you'll know something happened. Use the same procedure. Is that a roger?"

"It's a roger," Lily said.

We slowed as we passed the first house on Chaparral Road. It was actually off the road, up a short blacktop drive.

"We'll check this one out," I whispered. "But keep going till you find a good place to hide Big Red." There was no need to whisper, but whispering seemed appropriate. There was no place to hide Big Red, so we left it in full view but about a quarter mile up Chaparral Road.

Silence lay all around us, filling the valleys, shadowing the mountain slopes. I looked at my watch. Ten minutes to five. Sypey would be getting supper ready for the two of us. In another half hour she'd start worrying. I should have called her from the market and made up a time-delaying excuse.

Lily and I walked in the long, tufted grass at the side of the road, not talking, careful to make no sound. A thick, spiky bush at the end of the driveway made a perfect hiding place for Lily, though when I checked, one of her jaguar's eyes still showed. I suggested that when I was gone she turn the front to the back and be less conspicuous. Then I tucked my shirt neatly into my jeans, tightened my belt, and took out my detective notebook.

"For my chocolate orders," I whispered.

"Cluck if you need me," she whispered back.

The blacktop was warm through my tennies. I observed the house as I walked. It was old, ordinary, square-shaped. I couldn't figure out what a developer had fixed up. There was a cactus garden in front and an empty birdbath. The drapes were tightly drawn and nothing moved. A fence about six feet high joined the house and garage and stretched back, probably enclosing a backyard. Three steps went up to a porch, where a pot held a dead geranium. No sign of a blue tree. I pushed the bell, hearing it ring deep in the house. Nobody came. I rang again, rehearsing what I'd say. Again nobody came. Shoot! I thought. The place might even still be empty. Cross off the first house on Chaparral Road. But maybe I'd check around back, just to be sure.

The wooden gate in the fence had a string hanging down so you could open the latch from outside. I pulled it and went into the backyard.

There was nothing there but a square swimming pool set in the bare cement. Man! I held my nose. This place must definitely be empty. Who could live close to a pool like that? The water must be foul. I decided there had to be water under the thick green slime and the dead leaves and branches. I touched the top with the toe of my tenny. Yuk! The muck must have been an inch thick. Water oozed up around my laces, and a bunch of small black flies swarmed toward my face. I batted them away and whispered, "Git! Go! Get out of here!" The scum swayed and settled, and the flies went back to munching on it, or whatever they were doing. Gross City!

The side of the garage edged up against the fence. A ledge all the way around gave me a convenient toehold, so I boosted myself up and looked through the garage window. The inside was small, bare and empty. Dust danced in the rays of sun that spiked through the glass. I was just about to let myself down when I spotted something. On the cement floor were oil drops, each one abut the size of a quarter, three in a row, three in a row. I stared, telling myself that every car that ever had a motor leaked oil sometime or other. These drops meant nothing. But I wasn't listening to myself.

I got down, went back through the gate and tried the garage doors. There was a bolt and padlock but the lock lay open. I slid it free, and all the time I was listening, because now that I'd seen these quarter-sized drops, everything had changed. This wasn't just any house I was checking. It might be *the* house. And whoever lived in it, whoever parked his car in here, could come back at any minute.

It was hot and airless in the garage. I crouched, examining the spots, hoping I'd find tire tracks where someone had driven over the oil, but there were none. Maybe Sam Spade could have looked and known without a doubt that the oil was 200 weight, made by Pennzoil in 1989, cost three dollars a can, and was or was not the same as the oil in Lily's yard. I knew Jack Bull Diddley. Spade's next move would probably be to get inside the house. To gain entry. My heart did a double take. I wasn't sure if I could handle something that dangerous. Whatever Lily said, we had to hand this over to the police.

I tiptoed out of the garage, slid the bolt across and was just putting the padlock back the way I'd found it when I looked down.

A blue flower lay at my feet. But where had it come from?

I looked up. There was a tree in the overgrown yard next door. It was a green tree, thick with feathery, ferny leaves. But when I stood back and squinted I could see, right at the top, a scattering of pale-blue flowers.

"Jacaranda," I whispered. "Lily! How come you didn't see this?" But then I realized the angle of the house would hide it from where she was, behind the bush.

I was bending to pick up the flower when a voice spoke behind me. I think maybe I jumped six inches in the air, like a frog or something.

"Hey kid?" It was a young voice, a woman's,

friendly. There was a smile in it.

I straightened up and turned.

She was standing in the partly open door of the house, barefooted, wearing jeans and a navy-blue tank top. Her hair hung blond and straight below her shoulders. She was real tall.

"What were you looking for in our garage, my friend?"

My mind leaped this way and that. The chocolate story definitely was not going to wash. "I . . . I lost my cat," I said, squinting at her through the sun.

"That's too bad. What does he look like?"

"He's . . . he's Danish."

"A Danish cat?" She laughed. "That's a new one on me. What's his name? Bear Claw? Prune? You know, Prune Danish?"

"Ah . . . his name's Viking," I said.

"Viking. That's nice. Dignified. Well, if I see him I'll save him for you. Do you live around here?"

I nodded.

"And you thought your cat might just have

gotten locked in our garage?" she asked.

I nodded again, but I was thinking, Uh-oh. By now I figured she'd forgotten about the cat.

"Ouch," she said, and lifted one bare foot to examine it. "Just got a splinter."

"Those hurt," I said. I wanted to look back toward the bush to see if Lily was observing this. I hoped she was and that she had the good sense to stay out of sight.

The woman was crooking her finger at me to come closer, still standing on one foot. "Come on, fess up. You weren't looking for your cat, you were going to rip us off, right? You were hoping there might be something in there that you could cash and carry, right?"

"No I wasn't!" I was moving closer to her, honestly insulted. What did she think I was? Behind her, through the partly opened door, I could see a room without furniture, cardboard boxes partly stacked one on top of the other and, upside down against the back wall, a wooden stork.

My heart seemed to stop. I don't know what

my face did, but it did something for sure. Maybe my eyes popped open and my mouth, too. Maybe I gasped. Whatever I did, it was a tip-off.

She was beside me before I could get my mind to accept what I had seen. She grabbed my arm and dragged me up the steps. One hand covered my mouth. I could see her face, grim, angry, not smiling anymore. Man, was she strong. Strong as a sumo wrestler. I tried to break away, to kick at her shins. I tried to pull her hand away from my mouth so I could yell. I tried to bite but I couldn't. She yanked me inside the house, slammed the door and threw me across the room the same way someone would throw a Frisbee. I landed sitting right side up beside the upside-down stork. All of that and I hadn't even clucked.

CHAPTER SEVEN

She towered over me . . . Amazon lady, Viking. Her legs were planted as if she might lift an axe and bring it down to chop off my head.

"You saw the stork, didn't you?"

I tried to keep my face blank. I remember Sam Spade once getting out of a fix when "his face was stupid in its calmness." But it didn't seem to be working for me. I might be stupid, but I sure wasn't calm.

"That stork person's your mother, isn't she?" the Amazon asked.

"Who . . . who?" I sounded like some sick old owl.

"What do you mean, who?" She kicked my side, not hard, but hard enough. Big feet. I cringed back.

"You came looking for her, didn't you? You came to find your mother."

"I . . . I . . ." It was awful. I had started to blubber. Me, a detective. Sam Spade would have thrown up. The blubbering was all mixed up inside my head with being scared, and being caught. But most of all it was her saying, "You came to find your mother." It was because this awful woman must have known about my fantasy.

"I was selling chocolate," I began. "I mean, I was looking for my cat."

"Stop about the cat."

I stopped.

"Is anybody with you? You'd better tell the truth because I'm going to look, and if you lie, kid, you're in even bigger trouble."

There could be bigger trouble than this?

"There's nobody with me," I whispered, and I was thinking, Lily, Lily, please be gone. Please be halfway to the police station—or better still, all the way.

The Amazon pounced on me and dragged me along a corridor, my body bent over, my feet never catching up. At the end of the corridor was a door that she unbolted. One-handed she shoved me inside, into darkness. A light came on for a second, blinding me, shutting off again so suddenly that I wasn't sure if I'd seen what I thought I'd seen. I went tumbling down a flight of cement steps, stopping somehow before I got to the bottom, feeling with my hands for the step above or below. Feeling for anything.

The door banged shut and I heard the smooth heavy slide of the bolt.

"Are you okay?" The whispered words came from the woman in the basement below. I'd seen her in that one second of light.

She was moving toward me through the dark. Her hands guided mine. "Hold on to this railing. Are you badly hurt?"

"I don't think so."

"There are eight more steps. Can you make it?"

"Yes."

I came down on my butt, sliding the way a little kid would.

"Give me your hand," the woman said when I reached ground level. "There's nothing in here but a washer and dryer, and they're over on the other side. I thought there might have been a light in the dryer, but if there ever was, there isn't now."

I stumbled, holding on to her. One of us was limping, I wasn't sure which one.

"Here. Sit on the floor. There's a wall to lean against."

Above us a door slammed. "She's been outside," the woman said.

"Checking for Lily," I said.

"What? Oh no!" I felt her stiffen. "Lily's here, too?"

"Not anymore. She's gone to bring the police."

"You're sure?" she asked.

"Positive. You're her mother, aren't you?"

"Yes. But who are you? I don't understand."

"My name is Henry Coffin. I'm a friend of Lily's. We've been searching for you." I massaged my side where the Amazon lady had kicked me. "We were following the trail in the mileage book."

"They didn't get it, then? Thank goodness. I told them about the record I kept and that it was as good as a map and that it would lead the police right to them. I was trying to scare them into letting me go, Henry, and I would never, never have told where it was. But she twisted my arm and . . . so I told after all."

"Lily had already removed it, anyway," I said quickly. "No sweat. But why did they bring Big Red back in the first place?"

"There was no place to hide it. They argued. *She* thought it would make it look as if I'd gone home."

"Oh. Could you fill me in on the rest?"

Her voice was suddenly muffled, and I

sensed she'd covered her face with her hands. "You know how I sell my storks?"

"Yes."

"Kenny at the market told me . . ."

I interrupted. "I know about that, too."

"So I made two or three sweeps past these houses, and I was just about to give up when I saw this couple getting out of a car. The man, the father, was carrying a baby in one of those denim slings, like a backpack, only in front. Maybe they're called Snuglis?"

I didn't know what they were called, but I said, "Yes. Snuglis."

"The baby was wrapped in blankets. So I grabbed one of my storks and went up behind them."

There was a tiny rustling sound somewhere in the dark.

"Oh no!" Lily's mom shivered. "I think there are mice in here. Or snakes. I heard them all last night."

"That's okay," I said. "Mice and snakes are pretty nice. Honest. They won't hurt, unless it's a rattlesnake. And it'll warn you first."

"Thanks a lot!"

"Go on about the baby," I said.

"Well, when you're selling, it's good to say something nice, like 'Such beautiful eyes,' but I couldn't see its eyes or anything else, so I tweaked the blanket away from its face. The guy jumped forward and said, 'Don't you touch the baby.' But it was too late. I'd already seen."

"Seen what?"

"That it wasn't a baby. It was some sort of small statue of an old Chinese man, green jade, I think. I was just about to say 'Sorry,' and I was thinking what a strange way to carry an ornament, when the woman grabbed me, just grabbed me, and slammed me against the side of the house. They dragged me down here."

In spite of the dangerous situation and my own immediate peril, my trained detective's mind was whirling. "The statue must have been stolen. Valuable too. They were afraid you'd recognize it and tell." And then I remembered yesterday afternoon, my dad with his feet on the desk reading from THE POLICE BLOTTER. I was so excited I tried to leap up but my side hurt too bad. "It's a jade statue from the Ming Dynasty. *The Divine Scholar.* The paper had a picture of it, even. It was stolen from the Eastern Asia Museum two days ago, and it's worth a fortune. Somehow those two went into the exhibit and smuggled *The Divine Scholar* out in the Snugli thing, right past the guards. I can't believe it! When Sam Spade was looking for the Maltese Falcon, he went to the Fat Man and—"

"Sh!"

Above us the woman was talking. "She's making a phone call," Lily's mom whispered. "Probably to him. He went off in the the car this afternoon. If we listen hard, we'll be able to hear some of what she says. I think the phone must be right above us."

Words and fragments of sentences came clearly down.

". . . home right away . . . must have found . . ." Two or three times the name Crowley came through. "Crowley will pay . . ." A lot of silence, then: "No. To some rich collector." More silence. "Don't forget the plane tickets." Her voice dropped, but I could still get part of it. "Uh-uh. *She* saw both of us and *he* saw . . . Oh no! *I'm* not going to do it. . . . You have to." What? He had to do what? My heart was thumping so hard, I almost missed the last of it. "All right. See you in twenty minutes."

There was silence then and the padding of her feet again across the floor above.

"Twenty minutes," I whispered.

Mrs. Larson was whispering, too. "Could Lily be back by then with the police?"

"I don't know." But I did know. Twenty minutes wasn't very long.

"Oh, Henry," Lily's mom said in the saddest, saddest voice. "I'm so sorry we got you into this."

"I'm a detective," I said. "This is the way I

make my living." I'd always wanted to say that, but somehow it sounded fake. "We have to think!" I said. "There must be something we can do." I looked at the strip of pale light coming under the door at the top of the steps. "If we both threw ourselves against the door . . ."

"I've pushed. I've thumped. I promised them on my honor I'd never tell anybody about this or them, or the baby in the Snugli. She told me to be quiet or she'd shove a gag down my throat."

Upstairs a TV went on. The news. Five o'clock. Five thirty? Sypey would have called Paul by now. She'd be just starting to worry. Another hour and she'd be berserk, and she should be. By then we'd be dead meat. Don't fail me now, Sam.

"We've got to get her to open that door," I said. "But how? What about if you tell her I have a broken leg?"

"Sweetheart, she doesn't care if you have two broken legs."

I peered around, trying to see through the darkness. "You've checked that there aren't any hammers or . . . or electric saws . . . or . . ."

"There's nothing."

"The washer and dryer," I said quickly. "Do they work?"

"I didn't try doing laundry, if that's what you mean," she said. She could make a joke now! Of course, it was a pretty weak joke.

"I know that! Hurry! Take off your shoes!" I said.

"They're boots."

"Even better." I was unlacing my tennies. "Do you have a purse?"

"Yes. The woman upstairs took the wallet. She left me the rest."

"Bring the purse. Show me where the dryer is."

"Could you . . . Do you think you could help me get my boot off?" she asked. "There's something wrong with my ankle."

"Oh. Sure. I'm sorry, I didn't know."

She groaned as I pulled at the heel and the toe. Once she said, "Stop! Oh, please stop for a minute."

"I'm sorry," I said again.

"Oh, man!" she breathed when I finally got it off. I thought maybe she was crying. I waited for a few seconds, then said, "You stay right here. Point me in the right direction and I'll come back and help you."

She came behind me, though.

I found the two machines and ran my hands over their shiny smoothness, trying to decide which was which. This was the dryer. I opened the front and soundlessly slid in her boots and my tennies.

"What have you got in your purse?"

"A hairbrush. Compact. A pen . . ."

She gave them to me one by one, and one by one I put them in. "I don't know if this will work," I said, "but it's worth a try."

There were some quarters and dimes in my pocket, and I put them in with the rest of the stuff.

"How about my belt?" Lily's mom asked. "It's a chain."

"Perfect." I pulled mine out of its loops too. It's leather, but it has a humongous buckle. "Do you know how to make the dryer go?"

"They're all about the same. There'll be a dial and a button to make it start." I heard her fingers scrambling across the enamel too.

"Don't push the button yet," I said. "I'm going to the top of the stairs. When I say 'Now!' start it. And pray it comes on. Just pray, because we don't have a trial run. When Sypey dries my sneaks, the noise is deafening. This should be worse. I'm hoping the Amazon will come to see what it is, and when she opens the door I'm going to try to grab her and shove her down the steps. I'll bolt the door and make a run for help."

I wished I could see her face. Talking to her and not seeing her was hard. "Of course, that means I have to leave you with her, down here, in the dark. I wish there was some other way, but one of us has to press the button." I felt around till I found her hand. "You could do the standing behind the door part. I could stay."

Her grasp tightened on mine. "I don't think I could shove anybody down steps, Henry. Not even her. You go. Good luck."

The steps were ice-cold under my socks as I went up them. My side ached as if I'd run too far, too fast. I pressed my ear to the door. The TV was still on. I recognized Tom Brokaw.

"Now," I said.

From down below, from out of the darkness—from out of the dryer, actually—came a thunderous thumping and clanking and clattering. And beyond the door, along the corridor, I heard the sound of bare feet running, running in my direction.

CHAPTER EIGHT

A light went on. I'd forgotten there would be a light and it almost threw me, but not quite. She flung open the door and I was one step down so it wouldn't knock me off balance.

"What's going on?" she shouted, and shouted no more. I grabbed her wrist and pulled with all my strength. She teetered there on the top step and I yanked again, pressing myself against the railing as she went past. One glance over my shoulder showed her rushing at top speed, her legs going like pistons, those big feet tripping her up. That same glance showed me Lily's mom crouched at the dryer. Then I was outside the door. I jammed the light switch off and shot the bolt across, then slid to my knees like some old Raggedy Andy doll with no bones to hold me up. I put my mouth to the crack in the door and called with all my strength, "You harm one hair of her head, Amazon woman, and you'll be ground sirloin . . . I promise. And I don't make rash promises."

No time to congratulate myself on the success of my plan or the tough way I'd talked. Sam Spade couldn't have done better.

I ran to the living room. There was the phone. I told my fingers to dial 911 and they did, but there was no sound. "Come on, come on," I whispered. Then I saw the dangling wire. She must have cut it, getting ready to leave. Okay. Out of here and fast.

The baby sling was by the front door and all set to go. I took one second to peel back the blanket and make sure who was wrapped so carefully inside. It was *The Divine Scholar*, all right. He smiled at me mysteriously, his face stupid in its calmness.

I put the sling around my front, holding him cradled below in case he'd bump something and crack. Man, he was heavy. I wouldn't be running too fast with him hanging around my neck. I could have left him, I suppose. But he was evidence. Rule Number 7 in the detective's handbook is: Never abandon evidence. I was having another problem, too. Without my belt my jeans kept slipping around my knees. I had to keep stopping to hitch them up. Darn that Sypey anyway. She always buys them too big so I can grow into them. Also because she says it's not healthy for a growing boy to wear tight pants.

I opened the door, surprised to see daylight. The basement had been dark as a tomb. A bunch of crows on a phone wire eyed me suspiciously and squawked: "Who are you?"

"Coffin," I yelled. "On a case."

I was just about at the end of the short blacktop when I heard a car coming. No siren, just a car. But the police could be sneaking up quietly. Maybe I could just stop someone and bum a ride to the nearest phone. Then I heard the loud music. The same kind the guy who drove Big Red had been playing. I looked around frantically, hiking up my pants. No place to hide. And he'd seen me. It was a blue Toyota, slowing, not slow enough to let me see if it was driving on snake tires. But I knew.

"Hey you!" The man called out the window. I got one glimpse of a pale face and pale hair, and then I was running, faster than light, back to the house. Amazing that I could move like this with *The Divine Scholar* like a lump of lead on my stomach and my pants halfway to my knees. Fear makes you fast. It was a new proverb and I'd invented it.

I'd go in the front door, bolt it, go in the bathroom, bolt that, too. I was panting worse than Maximillian. I wished we'd brought him. That was a serious mistake, leaving him.

Behind me the car came to a screeching stop, just below the steps. Its door slammed. By then I was in the living room, my head jerking from side to side like a puppet on a string. No place to hide. No couch, no chair, a TV on a box. His key in the lock. Run to the bathroom. But he was in the house too, not forty yards from me. I don't know forty yards, but I know he was close, closer than the bathroom door.

I raced through another door into a bedroom. No use hiding under the bed. It was the first place he'd look. The bare wooden floor was white with dust. A broom leaned against the wall. An overflowing dustpan sat next to it. Someone had started to clean up.

He was coming.

Maybe I could whack him with the broom? No, wait.

I grabbed the dustpan and made myself stand in front of the door, just where he'd come in.

The knob turned. He was there. Small. Not

much taller than I am. Glasses . . . blond hair.

For a millisecond I saw his surprise, then I threw the dust into his face.

He was hidden in a white swirling cloud. I couldn't see him but I could sure hear him. He was spluttering and coughing. I glanced back once as I ran for the window. He was doubled over as if he'd been kicked in the stomach.

The window drapes were closed. I jerked them open. A sliding glass door. Outside, the bare backyard.

The man was croaking at me.

"You little punk! You've blinded me!"

No time to stop and tell him how sorry I was.

I slid open the door and was outside.

Oh no! What now? No trees to climb. No bushes. I wished that jacaranda was in this yard. I wished I'd find a snake on the bare concrete—I'd throw it at him. I wished a shark would come snapping up from the foulness of the pool. I'd throw him at it. The man was yelling now. Wow, was he mad! "Come out from behind those drapes! When I get ahold of you, I'm going to . . ."

I didn't want to find out what he was going to do.

I was in the pool, sinking, sinking down into its crusted, slimy depths, *The Divine Scholar* bringing me with him to the bottom. I unhooked him from around my neck and set him gently in the drain circle where he couldn't rock around. Bubbles blew out of my nose. I had started to count off seconds, the way I do when I'm timing Paul underwater and timing myself to be sure I'm better. Forty-two, forty-three. I paddled under the mush to the chrome ladder that led from the deep end to the poolside. Chrome? It was green and covered with long, waving grass. Nice. Fifty-three, fifty-four. I was busting my own record. I was busting my lungs, too.

I came up faster than I should have, hand over hand on the slippery ladder. Maybe I'd get the bends. The top of my head broke the skim of slime and I gasped for breath, but softly. I peered through a big hunk of withered palm frond that lay in the solid surface. Uh-oh. The guy was in the yard, too, standing on the fence ledge looking into the garage just the way I'd done.

"Where are you, you brat?" he yelled.

The gate into the yard swung back and forth. I think maybe I'd left it open when I came in before. He turned toward it, his head poked forward on his neck. Then he got down from the ledge and tiptoed over to the gate. I slid down so no part of me was above water but my eyes and nose. I must have looked like a small hippopotamus browsing in the dirtiest pool in the jungle. Sypey would have had a heart attack if she'd seen what was around me. She won't even let me drink faucet water. "Microbes, Henry!" This pool would give her microbes, all right.

I could see his back. He was staring both ways along Chaparral Road. I took another deep breath and sank. One, two, three, four.

I came up at fifty-four, ready to explode. The yard was empty. Where? Where? Too dangerous to get out.

There were voices from the front of the house now. His and the Amazon's. The Amazon's was wicked with rage. "He got past you somehow! He has the *Scholar*. You sure managed to mess everything up!"

"*I* messed everything up! Who let a kid lock her in the basement? Who . . . ?"

"He can't have gone far. Get moving."

"Which way?"

"Oh, for heaven's . . ."

Car doors slammed and I couldn't hear whatever else they said. I waited till the sound of the motor disappeared before I pulled myself out of the pool. There was moss or something all over me. I hoped it hadn't taken root. Seaweed hung from my hair. I picked it out. It wasn't seaweed. I didn't want to know what it really was. *The Divine Scholar* was still down there in the drain. I hoped his jade could stand it. He might be greener when he came out than when he went in. But I knew one thing: I wasn't going back for him.

The crows were still on the telephone wires.

I held my arms out and spread my fingers and walked toward them on stiffened legs. "I am the creature from the black lagoon," I told them and they took off, every single one of them. I was halfway back to the bedroom window when I heard a whining sound. At first I worried that it was water in my ears, which wasn't a pleasant worry. What if that stuff leaked up into my brain? I tipped my head to let it run out and realized it wasn't water. It was the lovely, happy sound of police sirens.

Jack Aquino hadn't been in the station when Lily got there. But the other officers had believed her. "See?" I said. "Doesn't that restore your faith in them?"

Lily sniffed. "I hope it restores theirs in me."

Mrs. Larson had to be carried up from

101

the basement on stretcher because she had a broken ankle.

"This is nothing compared to what might have happened to us if it hadn't been for Henry," she said.

She and Lily wanted to pay me, but I said, Never. Helping them was payment enough.

When I told Paul later that I'd turned down money, he said I was so dumb I must have been hatched from a turtle egg.

A police diver brought *The Divine Scholar* up from the bottom of the pool. He wore a mask and wet suit.

"Wimps," I whispered to Lily.

"You ever hear of jaundice, kid?" he snarled at me.

"Uh, no."

"Your skin turns yellow and you look like a banana."

"Don't worry. He's just mad at you for calling him a wimp," Lily whispered.

I did worry, though.

The police got the Amazon and her

mate—they hadn't gone far, and Mrs. Larson and I were right there to make the identification two days later.

The *Morning Star* did a whole feature on me, complete with pictures of the mayor giving me a commendation and pictures of *The Divine Scholar* and me—at least one of us looking like a million dollars.

"Nah!" Paul said when he read the article. "You never stayed down in that pool for no fifty-four seconds. You couldn't. Did you count?"

I could tell he was anxious about the underwater swim competition.

"I counted," I said. "But you know how time flies when you're having fun."

My dad and George Pale were real proud of me, and Sypey baked a cake to celebrate and invited Lily and Mrs. Larson. The cake was made from raw sugar, egg whites and cholesterol-lowering soy flour. I thought it tasted pretty good, which probably shows that my taste buds are losing it. Lily sat next to me on the couch and kept telling everyone how brave I was and asking her mom to describe again the way I'd pulled the Amazon down the basement stairs.

Sypey went "tut tut" at that and looked disapproving, but she offered me another piece of health cake, so I knew things were okay. I was hoping Dad and Mrs. Larson might like each other, which would have been nice, but my detective's intuition told me that wasn't going to happen. As Sam might say, "You can't make it go the way it doesn't want to go."

I was also hoping that my mom would read about me and come home at last. But that didn't happen either. So I guess it's just me and Dad and Sypey. Which isn't so bad, really. But I'm not ready yet to let go of my fantasy. That's the best thing about a fantasy. You don't have to let go of it, ever.

Now that junior high's started, Lily picks me up a couple of days a week in Big Red. Sometimes, if I'm late, she waits for me, sitting on the hood, swinging her little white boots. Talk

out status! Man, I could be president of sev-
th grade if I wanted . . . of the whole school,
en.

And there's another good thing: I check myself every morning. And so far I haven't turned
into a banana.